PRAISE FOR M. L. BUCHMAN

A fabulous soaring thriller.

— *TAKE OVER AT MIDNIGHT,* MIDWEST BOOK REVIEW

Meticulously researched, hard-hitting, and suspenseful.

— *PURE HEAT,* PUBLISHERS WEEKLY, STARRED REVIEW

Expert technical details abound, as do realistic military missions with superb imagery that will have readers feeling as if they are right there in the midst and on the edges of their seats.

— *LIGHT UP THE NIGHT,* RT REVIEWS, 4 1/2 STARS

Buchman has catapulted his way to the top tier of my favorite authors.

— FRESH FICTION

Nonstop action that will keep readers on the edge of their seats.

— *TAKE OVER AT MIDNIGHT,* LIBRARY JOURNAL

M L. Buchman's ability to keep the reader right in the middle of the action is amazing.

— LONG AND SHORT REVIEWS

The only thing you'll ask yourself is, "When does the next one come out?"

— *WAIT UNTIL MIDNIGHT,* RT REVIEWS, 4 STARS

The first...of (a) stellar, long-running (military) romantic suspense series.

— *THE NIGHT IS MINE,* BOOKLIST, "THE 20 BEST ROMANTIC SUSPENSE NOVELS: MODERN MASTERPIECES"

I knew the books would be good, but I didn't realize how good.

— NIGHT STALKERS SERIES, KIRKUS REVIEWS

Buchman mixes adrenalin-spiking battles and brusque military jargon with a sensitive approach.

— PUBLISHERS WEEKLY

13 times "Top Pick of the Month"

— NIGHT OWL REVIEWS

Tom Clancy fans open to a strong female lead will clamor for more.

— *DRONE*, PUBLISHERS WEEKLY

Superb! Miranda is utterly compelling!

— *BOOKLIST,* STARRED REVIEW

Miranda Chase continues to astound and charm.

— BARB M.

Escape Rating: A. Five Stars! OMG just start with *Drone* and be prepared for a fantastic binge-read!

— READING REALITY

The best military thriller I've read in a very long time. Love the female characters.

— *DRONE,* SHELDON MCARTHUR,
FOUNDER OF THE MYSTERY
BOOKSTORE, LA

BODY MEMORY

A SCIENCE FICTION ROMANCE

M. L. BUCHMAN

Originally published in *Pulphouse Magazine* 2018

Receive a free book and discover more by this author at: www.mlbuchman.com

Cover images:

Future Man © rolffimages

Other works by M. L. Buchman: *(* - also in audio)*

Action-Adventure Thrillers

Dead Chef

One Chef!
Two Chef!

Miranda Chase

*Drone**
*Thunderbolt**
*Condor**
*Ghostrider**
*Raider**
*Chinook**
*Havoc**
*White Top**
*Start the Chase**
*Lightning**
*Skibird**
*Nightwatch**
*Osprey**
*Gryphon**

Science Fiction / Fantasy

Deities Anonymous

Cookbook from Hell: Reheated
Saviors 101

Contemporary Romance

Eagle Cove

Return to Eagle Cove
Recipe for Eagle Cove
Longing for Eagle Cove
Keepsake for Eagle Cove

Love Abroad

Heart of the Cotswolds: England
Path of Love: Cinque Terre, Italy

Where Dreams

Where Dreams are Born
Where Dreams Reside
*Where Dreams Are of Christmas**
Where Dreams Unfold
Where Dreams Are Written
Where Dreams Continue

Non-Fiction

Strategies for Success

Managing Your Inner Artist/Writer
*Estate Planning for Authors**
Character Voice
*Narrate and Record Your Own Audiobook**
Beyond Prince Charming: One Guy's Guide to Writing Men in Romance

Short Story Series by M. L. Buchman:

Action-Adventure Thrillers

Dead Chef

Miranda Chase Stories

Romantic Suspense

Antarctic Ice Fliers

US Coast Guard

Contemporary Romance

Eagle Cove

Other

Deities Anonymous (fantasy)

Single Titles

The Emily Beale Universe
(military romantic suspense)

The Night Stalkers
MAIN FLIGHT
The Night Is Mine
I Own the Dawn
Wait Until Dark
Take Over at Midnight
Light Up the Night
Bring On the Dusk
By Break of Day
Target of the Heart
Target Lock on Love
Target of Mine
Target of One's Own
NIGHT STALKERS HOLIDAYS
*Daniel's Christmas**
*Frank's Independence Day**
*Peter's Christmas**
Christmas at Steel Beach
*Zachary's Christmas**
*Roy's Independence Day**
*Damien's Christmas**
Christmas at Peleliu Cove

Henderson's Ranch
*Nathan's Big Sky**
*Big Sky, Loyal Heart**
*Big Sky Dog Whisperer**
*Tales of Henderson's Ranch**

Shadow Force: Psi
*At the Slightest Sound**
*At the Quietest Word**
*At the Merest Glance**
*At the Clearest Sensation**

White House Protection Force
*Off the Leash**
*On Your Mark**
*In the Weeds**

Firehawks
Pure Heat
Full Blaze
*Hot Point**
*Flash of Fire**
Wild Fire
SMOKEJUMPERS
*Wildfire at Dawn**
*Wildfire at Larch Creek**
*Wildfire on the Skagit**

Delta Force
*Target Engaged**
*Heart Strike**
*Wild Justice**
*Midnight Trust**

Emily Beale Universe Short Story Series

The Night Stalkers
The Night Stalkers Stories
The Night Stalkers CSAR
The Night Stalkers Wedding Stories
The Future Night Stalkers

Delta Force
Th Delta Force Shooters
The Delta Force Warriors

Firehawks
The Firehawks Lookouts
The Firehawks Hotshots
The Firebirds

White House Protection Force
Stories

Future Night Stalkers
Stories (Science Fiction)

ABOUT THIS BOOK

He remembers her. Her touch, her scent, the way her glance could make his heart race. His very body remembers her though she is long gone.

Until his job began to grind it away, one small memory at a time.

WHY I WROTE THIS STORY

THIS STORY IS ACTUALLY A KIND OF LOVE SONNET TO MY wife. We didn't meet until we both well along the way. But even after a quarter century together, I can still remember the first time we touched. And kissed. And held hands as we walked—we still do whenever the sidewalk is wide enough.

People live and learn in different ways. Some are visually focused, some auditory, and yet others by taste and smell. My best learning path is touch (which wasn't exactly useful in school but would explain a lot of why I was so much better at Geology than Physics.

Being kinesthetic, touch-focused, I swear that I can remember every little thing this story's hero does about his wife.

It began as a writing challenge. "Here's a scientific article about a new technology called biotubes. Write a romance using that." So, I did.

BODY MEMORY

I WAS THIRTY-SEVEN WHEN THE FIRST PIECE OF MY BODY went missing. That was older than most who made their living climbing out of Earth's deep gravity well three times a week. Side of my aorta blew out at about four gees. The meddies were ready for it. Sent the clamp-down signal to my suit, pumped me full of enough juice to let me keep riding the controls all the way up to Main Street.

Blow-outs weren't all that unusual. As long as it didn't tear up the whole heart, they didn't lose a pilot very often anymore. But it was the only time we ever got more attention than our cargo, a rare event at the primary receiving station in LEO.

Low Earth Orbit was always a total snarl, nothing unusual there. Main Station Redistribution Terminal, Main Street, was the busiest and most important station in the whole solar system. Unable to track all of the whirling space junk clogging up most orbits, they'd chosen to defend one corridor up to Main Street, that one station, and one corridor outbound. I got the *Caroline* docked, then they pulled me.

They slipped into me with the precision of long practice, not even cracking my chest the way they did as recently as a dozen years ago. They burrowed in with long, thin tools, clipped out the blown bits of my aorta, and put in the new biotube. Some other tech had punched through to my bone marrow and extracted some cells to swipe over the synth tubing. I'd be two weeks in the sling while the cells grew and the tube biodegraded. Two months doing zero-gee piloting, and two more doing the low-grav stuff to the moon or Mars before they'd recertify me for the lucrative Earth-launch seat.

After twelve years of punching it hard up into the blue sky, I could do with a break.

At first I thought it was the drugs. Can't be moving around in the first two weeks, so they kept me pretty doped. Didn't feel much of anything which is always fine when it's happening. The drugs don't let you worry much.

Something was missing though, it just took me a while to find it. I was on the deadman stretch back from Phobos shipyard around Mars. It was a long slide back down-system to Earth without much to do.

I was never a deep man. Some of the long-haulers read or learned a language. Some wrote stories or studied for some degree that would serve them when they tired of the stark beauty of driving across the unending sky. Though no one ever did.

I tend to just drift. Watch a few vids, read a bit of

trade, but mostly I just watch the black and the unmoving stars. And I drift.

Sometimes those drifting thoughts take me places that are good, sometimes not, but I figure that too is like life. I lost my Caroline five years after I named my ship for her. We were one of those clichés, the kind they don't even put in the sitcoms 'cause no one would believe it. She was the blond beauty from up the road. The older woman who captured my heart when I was six and she was seven.

We never needed anyone else. From the sandbox to my first lift into space, the two of us were always enough together. Enough? We were all that mattered to each other.

The cancer took her so fast I never had time to grieve. Not many pilots took three launches a week, but once I no longer had any reason to stay on the ground, I flew. I didn't grieve, but I did remember.

So, a lot of the time on those deep crossings, I'd spend thinking of Caroline. The good with the bad. But there was so much good, it wasn't hard spending most of my time there.

It was on that last long crossing after four months of light work, that I found what was missing. When I thought of Caroline, my heart no longer sped up in remembered hope, anticipation, desire. The busted-heart had been proof of my ultimate mortality. It brought me a little closer to understanding that I was fallible, that I was human. That I, like Caroline, could also die.

While I felt closer to her for that awareness, somehow my new heart felt a little farther away from her as well.

THE NEXT PIECE OF MY BODY WENT MISSING AT FIFTY-TWO after sticking with me for another fifteen years. It was both a funny and a stupid way to lose a hand.

After the third cardio-blowout took a big chunk of my heart with it, they booted me permanently off the BSL. The Beesel, Blue Sky Launch, was a young man's game anyway. I now live permanently in the N-Sky. For most Night Skyers, the only atmosphere we'll ever see again is the pink of Mars, and the terraformers still have a long way to go before I'd be able to breathe there without a suit. If I go back to Earth's surface, they tell me I won't be able to climb the gravity-well again. Not on hard fuel, not on mag-lev rail launch—ever.

That's okay by me. It's not a lonely life; there are a lot of lifers in the N-Sky. Only a few of us can't return, most others just don't want to. They're happy with the rock they've chosen or the few who enjoy flying between them like I do. The deep spacers with no homes but our ships, we're the warriors of the N-Sky.

The thing that was stupid about losing my hand, was forgetting how the world worked. Inside my ship, I was the heaviest thing to move around by a factor of about a hundred. Outside my ship, I was one of the smallest things you could imagine; ships, satellites, moons, planets, meteors, and the like made my puny mass wholly insignificant.

I normally sat inside while taking on a load, but I was out smoothing filler into the inevitable holes that micrometeors and space dust punched in my comm dish.

Once every six months, I'd go paste up the worst of them to keep my signals hot. So there I was when some young buck stevedore got a load of hydroponic gear moving into my cargo bay, but missed the insertion angle by two full degrees. How that's even possible I still don't know.

Instinctively reaching out to stop a thousand-kilo load from crushing my fresh-patched antenna was about as dumb as you could get. It didn't even tear my suit, just flattened my hand thinner than a viewpad. With no breach, I had to manually trigger my suit's meds before my screams blew out my own ears inside my helmet.

They grew me a new hand. The skin took a while and the bones were a carbon-silicate of some sort, but the rest of it was me. Lotta little biotubes and other tricks, but it was me.

The news was all full of noise about bioengineered regeneration being the road to immortality. It wasn't in finding the still-elusive longevity gene, immortality was in convincing the body to replace parts of itself. So, in some ways, my heart was fifteen years younger than the rest of me, except my hand was the youngest of all, barely three months old the next time I pulled the repaired and upgraded *Caroline* away from Main Street.

It felt younger too. Perhaps it really was. Newer nerves, newer muscles, ceramic joints—that is once I got them conditioned through all the physical therapy. My reaction time had even gone up. Not a lot, just to the speed of my younger days. I'd lost some things over the years: response time, dexterity, tactile sensitivity. Those came back.

But the years had cost me more than that.

They'd cost me the memory of how it felt to brush a tear from Caroline's cheek as she tried again to apologize for leaving me so soon. I'd lost the memory of how her hand felt in mine when we walked the long ocean beaches down where Philadelphia had once been.

IT WAS ANOTHER FORTY YEARS BEFORE I TRIED BREATHING the hard vacuum of space. It wasn't intentional. A stray piece of space junk glanced off my visor—which shattered and was gone.

I'd been working outside-ship with a small team patching a satellite when an old steering jet nozzle lost fifty years before found me. By the time they had me inside and repressurized, I'd iced my eyes, ears, mouth, and lungs. Oddly enough, it was the intense sunburn from three full minutes of exposure to the Sun's UV radiation that hurt the worst.

The regrowth took time, but the process wasn't painful.

Except for what I lost.

THIRTY MORE YEARS HAVE COME AND GONE SINCE THEN.

I've talked to a lot of other spacers, both the Beesel and the N-sky. Chatted with shrinks in Main Street bars and neurologists in quiet corners out at Europa Station with Jupiter looming larger than God outside the viewports.

They think I'm going senile.

Calcified brain, they declare. The tests concur. Needs a replacement.

I have a theory, that no one but me believes, yet I know now to be true. These young cells, these new parts of me that extend my life, they never knew Caroline. They can no longer taste her lips, smell her skin, revel in her trickling laugh. The hand never knew that the side of her breast and the curve of her cheek were of the exact same softness. The new heart never raced at the mere thought of her.

Maybe no one else ever had what I had, so none have lost what I lost. No one but me ever had a Caroline to lose.

They told me my new brain will remember everything; they can finally do that.

I know better now.

My new brain is a young one.

It doesn't remember how it *felt* to be so loved.

Wish I'd figured all this while it still mattered.

AFTERWORD

If you enjoyed this
please consider leaving a review.
They really help.

Keep reading for an exciting excerpt from:
Miranda Chase #13, Osprey

Be sure to visit:
https://mlbuchman.com/fan-club-freebies

- *Bonus Scene/Story for the novels*
- *Recipes from the books*
- *Character list, place maps, plane pictures, and more*

COME VISIT: THE WORLDS OF M. L.

SIX TALES IN SIX WORLDS

THE GODS ARE OUT INN (EXCERPT)

TUESDAY MORNING

"THAT DOESN'T LOOK LIKE A BEER AND A BUMP." MICHELLE glared at the glass Henrietta set atop the battered oaken bar and tried to figure out what it *did* look like. The light was dim enough that it was hard to see exactly what it was, but it definitely wasn't a beer and bump.

There was a general blueness to the drink—like a glass full of Windex—that was likely to be Curacao, an orange-flavored and typically bitter liqueur. Floating about in it were balls of red that weren't cherries, but might have been congealed Campari, an herbaceous liqueur that was also bitter. The deep-red globules slowly rose and fell in blue Curacao as if they were...

"It looks like sunsets," Henrietta's tiny expression was round-eyed with wonder as she gazed into the curvaceous Hurricane glass that overtopped her by several inches. "Don't you just love sunsets? I do and who wants a beer and a shot of whiskey when they can have sunsets? Really, Michelle. You must have more imagination. Look, see, now they're rising now. Sunrises!" Her voice practically squeaked with joy.

The foot-tall angel was so pleased that her wings lifted her several inches off the bar for a moment. Once she landed, she took one last admiring glance at her creation, then walked down the bar to serve the latest arrival. As she walked along, she gathered up Michelle's scattered peanut shells and stood up on her tiptoes to tip them into an empty bowl.

Michelle sipped at the drink reluctantly and it felt as if her face—her entire head—was trying to shrivel into one giant pucker. She hadn't noticed the thin layer of pure lemon juice that floated atop the Curacao. It must represent light gray clouds or some such; Henrietta hadn't explained and now that she was on to other things, there would be no point in asking either. The drink was surprisingly close to sucking on a bitter lemon.

Michelle took another cautious taste and decided that it wasn't quite as bad as that but it was close. Maybe she was getting used to it. She poked at a rising sun of Campari with her straw and sucked it dry. With its center gone, it imploded, much as a black hole would. The combination of the bitterness of a burned-out sun, the cosmic power to collapse it, and the high alcohol content was growing on her.

Of course, being the Devil Incarnate, she was used to wielding cosmic power, even if she was here in this bar trying to forget that.

"Hey!" The newcomer called out. "Come back here. This isn't what I ordered."

Michelle looked up to see her old friend Freyja

glaring down at her drink as Henrietta fluttered off to check on one of the tables. Michelle glanced up to make sure the ceiling fans weren't running—Henrietta had never really understood fans and would often get sucked up into them and have to be extracted. There was nothing in all creation worse than a dizzy angel with a speed-talking disorder.

"What did she give you?"

Freyja scowled down at her glass causing her long sun-blond tresses to fall down and cover her perfect breasts; the mortal artists had always rendered her naked from the waist up and now she was stuck with the look.

Michelle and Joshua the One God had been around since before the boot-up of the Software That Ran the Universe fourteen billion years ago and she'd thankfully avoided the whole horns, red skin, and tail thing that mortals came up with later—though there were times that she thought a tail might have been fun. Still, she was happy with the Amazonian body that made men—mortal and not—weep, long dark curly hair that curled too much when it was humid, and her own choices for clothing, mostly from the Levi's store.

"Hard apple cider," Freyja grimaced as she took another sip. "I am not Iounn—no matter what Richard Wagner said in the Ring operas. I am not the keeper of the golden apples of youth. I am the Norse goddess of sex, war, and death. I don't *want* hard apple cider. I don't *li*—"

"Have you ever won an argument with Henrietta?"

Freyja sighed and took a sip of her hard cider, "No. But I hate apples."

"I'll trade you," not that Michelle was a big fan of hard cider either, but the Norse goddess looked as if she'd had a hard day.

Keeping reading the story for free
By signing up for M. L.'s newsletter
at https://mlbuchman.com/newletter-sign-up

Or explore the site at:
https://mlbuchman.com

ABOUT THE AUTHOR

USA Today and Amazon #1 Bestseller M. L. "Matt" Buchman started writing on a flight south from Japan to ride his bicycle across the Australian Outback. Just part of a solo around-the-world trip that ultimately launched his writing career.

From the very beginning, his powerful female heroines insisted on putting character first, *then* a great adventure. He's since written over 75 action-adventure thrillers and military romantic suspense novels. And more than 200 short stories, and a fast-growing pile of read-by-author audiobooks.

PW declares of his Miranda Chase action-adventure thrillers: "Tom Clancy fans open to a strong female lead will clamor for more." About his military romantic thrillers: "Like Robert Ludlum and Nora Roberts had a book baby."

His fans say: "I want more now...of everything!" That his characters are even more insistent than his fans is a hoot. He is also the founder and editor of *Thrill Ride – the Magazine.*

As a 30-year project manager with a geophysics degree who has designed and built houses, flown and jumped out of planes, and solo-sailed a 50' ketch, he is awed by what is possible. He and his wife presently live on the North Shore of Massachusetts. More at: www.mlbuchman.com.

Other works by M. L. Buchman: *(* - also in audio)*

Action-Adventure Thrillers

Dead Chef

One Chef!
Two Chef!

Miranda Chase

*Drone**
*Thunderbolt**
*Condor**
*Ghostrider**
*Raider**
*Chinook**
*Havoc**
*White Top**
*Start the Chase**
*Lightning**
*Skibird**
*Nightwatch**
*Osprey**
*Gryphon**

Science Fiction / Fantasy

Deities Anonymous

Cookbook from Hell: Reheated
Saviors 101

Contemporary Romance

Eagle Cove

Return to Eagle Cove
Recipe for Eagle Cove
Longing for Eagle Cove
Keepsake for Eagle Cove

Love Abroad

Heart of the Cotswolds: England
Path of Love: Cinque Terre, Italy

Where Dreams

Where Dreams are Born
Where Dreams Reside
*Where Dreams Are of Christmas**
Where Dreams Unfold
Where Dreams Are Written
Where Dreams Continue

Non-Fiction

Strategies for Success

Managing Your Inner Artist/Writer
*Estate Planning for Authors**
Character Voice
*Narrate and Record Your Own Audiobook**
Beyond Prince Charming: One Guy's Guide to Writing Men in Romance

Short Story Series by M. L. Buchman:

Action-Adventure Thrillers

Dead Chef

Miranda Chase Stories

Romantic Suspense

Antarctic Ice Fliers

US Coast Guard

Contemporary Romance

Eagle Cove

Other

Deities Anonymous (fantasy)

Single Titles

The Emily Beale Universe
(military romantic suspense)

The Night Stalkers
MAIN FLIGHT
The Night Is Mine
I Own the Dawn
Wait Until Dark
Take Over at Midnight
Light Up the Night
Bring On the Dusk
By Break of Day
Target of the Heart
Target Lock on Love
Target of Mine
Target of One's Own
NIGHT STALKERS HOLIDAYS
*Daniel's Christmas**
*Frank's Independence Day**
*Peter's Christmas**
Christmas at Steel Beach
*Zachary's Christmas**
*Roy's Independence Day**
*Damien's Christmas**
Christmas at Peleliu Cove

Henderson's Ranch
*Nathan's Big Sky**
*Big Sky, Loyal Heart**
*Big Sky Dog Whisperer**
*Tales of Henderson's Ranch**

Shadow Force: Psi
*At the Slightest Sound**
*At the Quietest Word**
*At the Merest Glance**
*At the Clearest Sensation**

White House Protection Force
*Off the Leash**
*On Your Mark**
*In the Weeds**

Firehawks
Pure Heat
Full Blaze
*Hot Point**
*Flash of Fire**
Wild Fire
SMOKEJUMPERS
*Wildfire at Dawn**
*Wildfire at Larch Creek**
*Wildfire on the Skagit**

Delta Force
*Target Engaged**
*Heart Strike**
*Wild Justice**
*Midnight Trust**

Emily Beale Universe Short Story Series

The Night Stalkers
The Night Stalkers Stories
The Night Stalkers CSAR
The Night Stalkers Wedding Stories
The Future Night Stalkers

Delta Force
Th Delta Force Shooters
The Delta Force Warriors

Firehawks
The Firehawks Lookouts
The Firehawks Hotshots
The Firebirds

White House Protection Force
Stories

Future Night Stalkers
Stories (Science Fiction)

www.ingramcontent.com/pod-product-compliance
Lightning Source LLC
LaVergne TN
LVHW020313110826
845148LV00017BA/2666

* 9 7 8 1 6 3 7 2 1 1 5 2 6 *